This book is dedicated to every parent, educator, family member, and family friend who desires to see the children in their lives delight in reading.

"I Love Being Me!" That's the motto of Dudley Magnificent and the driving force behind the series. I believe that relatable, age-appropriate stories are a great resource to promote confidence and self-awareness. I have made it my mission to encourage children to celebrate the small everyday experiences that bring them happiness while reinforcing positive themes such as family, fun adventures, and unconditional love.

Thank you for your ongoing support.

Happy reading,

Michelle

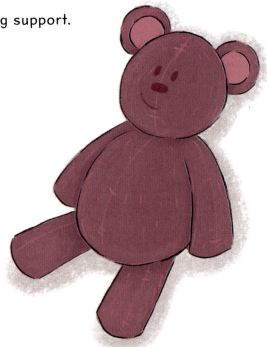

Dudley Magnificent presents:

Take Dudley to WORK DAY

To My loving husband Erik and amazing son Malcolm - M.E.F

Dudley Magnificent Presents: Take Dudley To Work Day

Copyright © 2020 by Lucid Hills Publications
All rights reserved. No part of this book may be reproduced, distributed, or transmitted in any form or by any means, including photocopying, recording or other electronic or mechanical methods,
without written permission
of the copyright owner. Except in the case of brief quotations embodied in reviews and certain other non-commercial uses.
Printed in the US
ISBN: 978-1-7323021-2-9

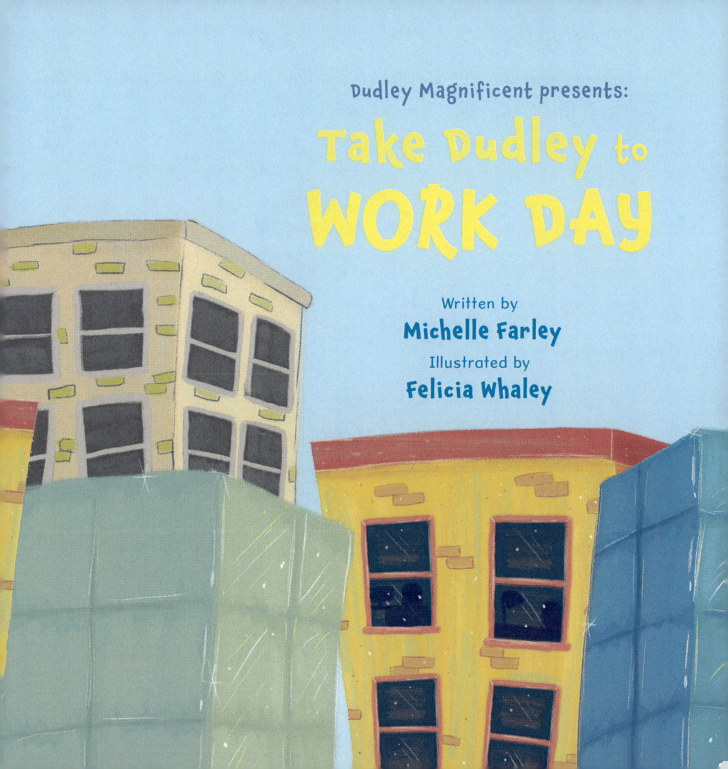

"Good night, Dudley. We have a big day planned for tomorrow," says Dudley's dad.

Guess what? Tomorrow, I'll get to be just like Daddy.

I'm going to shower and dress just like him.

We're going to eat breakfast and read the news together...
"More juice, Buddy?"
"Yes, please!"

We'll drive to work and look at all the tall buildings.

I'll get to walk through the revolving door.

I can't wait to ride the elevator and see all the grown-ups.

I'm going to say, "Good morning," and wave just like Daddy.

Daddy will help me push the elevator button for the top floor.

I'll have meetings, just like Daddy.

At lunchtime we'll sit outside.

Later, I'll write important messages, just like Daddy,

and make fun charts, too!

After work, we'll stop for root beer floats before grabbing takeout for dinner.

We'll even pick up flowers for Mommy.

Then, we'll sing songs in the car our entire ride home.

When Mommy comes home, we'll surprise her with dinner and flowers.

I'm going to tell Mommy all about my big day, and how I got to be just like Daddy.

Yep, tomorrow will be the best day ever.

About Michelle E. Farley

Michelle Elaine Farley wrote her first short story at seven years old and has been creating stories ever since. After receiving a BA from Cleveland State University and an MFA from National University, she taught student expository writing at the middle school, high school, and college level. She created the "Dudley Magnificent" series after noticing a lack of age-appropriate books for early young readers (0-5 years old) with an African American protagonist.

Her desire is not just to write entertaining children's books but also to create a community where young children can fall in love with reading.

Michelle is also an award-winning filmmaker, owner of an independent publishing company, 'Lucid Hills Publications', and a celebrated, professional copywriter that has helped hundreds of entrepreneurs and brands share their unique stories for optimal impact and influence.

Stay Connected!

Please consider taking a few minutes of your time to leave a book review. Visit **www.dudleymagnificentbooks.com** or **Amazon**. Reviews help other parents discover the Dudley Magnificent series and provides feedback about your book reading experience.

Visit **https://www.dudleymagnificentbooks.com** and sign-up for our email list.

Would you like Michelle to speak at your next program or event?

email: **michelle@dudleymagnificentbooks.com**.

Made in the USA
Las Vegas, NV
02 January 2022